The first...of (a) stellar, long-running (military) romantic suspense series.

I knew the books would be good, but I didn't realize how good.

Buchman mixes adrenalin-spiking battles and brusque military jargon with a sensitive approach.

13 times "Top Pick of the Month"

I0533073

PRAISE FOR M. L. BUCHMAN

Tom Clancy fans open to a strong female lead will clamor for more.

— *DRONE*, PUBLISHERS WEEKLY

Superb!

— *DRONE*, BOOKLIST STARRED REVIEW

The best military thriller I've read in a very long time. Love the female characters.

— *DRONE*, SHELDON MCARTHUR, FOUNDER OF THE MYSTERY BOOKSTORE, LA

A fabulous soaring thriller.

— *TAKE OVER AT MIDNIGHT*, MIDWEST BOOK REVIEW

Meticulously researched, hard-hitting, and suspenseful.

— *PURE HEAT*, PUBLISHERS WEEKLY, STARRED REVIEW

Expert technical details abound, as do realistic military missions with superb imagery that will have readers feeling as if they are right there in the midst and on the edges of their seats.

— *LIGHT UP THE NIGHT,* RT REVIEWS, 4 1/2 STARS

Buchman has catapulted his way to the top tier of my favorite authors.

— FRESH FICTION

Nonstop action that will keep readers on the edge of their seats.

— *TAKE OVER AT MIDNIGHT,* LIBRARY JOURNAL

M L. Buchman's ability to keep the reader right in the middle of the action is amazing.

— LONG AND SHORT REVIEWS

The only thing you'll ask yourself is, "When does the next one come out?"

— *WAIT UNTIL MIDNIGHT,* RT REVIEWS, 4 STARS

EMILY'S FIRST FLIGHT

A NIGHT STALKERS 5D STORY

M. L. BUCHMAN

Buchman Bookworks

Other works by M. L. Buchman: *(* - also in audio)*

Action-Adventure Thrillers

Dead Chef
One Chef!
Two Chef!

Miranda Chase
Drone*
Thunderbolt*
Condor*
Ghostrider*

Romantic Suspense

Delta Force
Target Engaged*
Heart Strike*
Wild Justice*
Midnight Trust*

Firehawks
MAIN FLIGHT
Pure Heat
Full Blaze
Hot Point*
Flash of Fire*
Wild Fire
SMOKEJUMPERS
Wildfire at Dawn*
Wildfire at Larch Creek*
Wildfire on the Skagit*

The Night Stalkers
MAIN FLIGHT
The Night Is Mine
I Own the Dawn
Wait Until Dark
Take Over at Midnight
Light Up the Night
Bring On the Dusk
By Break of Day

AND THE NAVY
Christmas at Steel Beach
Christmas at Peleliu Cove
WHITE HOUSE HOLIDAY
Daniel's Christmas*
Frank's Independence Day*
Peter's Christmas*
Zachary's Christmas*
Roy's Independence Day*
Damien's Christmas*
5E
Target of the Heart
Target Lock on Love
Target of Mine
Target of One's Own

Shadow Force: Psi
At the Slightest Sound*
At the Quietest Word*
At the Merest Glance*
At the Clearest Sensation*

White House Protection Force
Off the Leash*
On Your Mark*
In the Weeds*

Contemporary Romance

Eagle Cove
Return to Eagle Cove
Recipe for Eagle Cove
Longing for Eagle Cove
Keepsake for Eagle Cove

Henderson's Ranch
Nathan's Big Sky*
Big Sky, Loyal Heart*
Big Sky Dog Whisperer*

Love Abroad
Heart of the Cotswolds: England
Path of Love: Cinque Terre, Italy

Other works by M. L. Buchman:

Contemporary Romance (cont)

Where Dreams
Where Dreams are Born
Where Dreams Reside
Where Dreams Are of Christmas*
Where Dreams Unfold
Where Dreams Are Written

Science Fiction / Fantasy

Deities Anonymous
Cookbook from Hell: Reheated
Saviors 101

Single Titles
The Nara Reaction
Monk's Maze
the Me and Elsie Chronicles

Non-Fiction

Strategies for Success
Managing Your Inner Artist/Writer
Estate Planning for Authors*
Character Voice
Narrate and Record Your Own
Audiobook*

Short Story Series by M. L. Buchman:

Romantic Suspense

Delta Force
Th Delta Force Shooters
The Delta Force Warriors

Firehawks
The Firehawks Lookouts
The Firehawks Hotshots
The Firebirds

The Night Stalkers
The Night Stalkers
The Night Stalkers 5E
The Night Stalkers CSAR
The Night Stalkers Wedding Stories

US Coast Guard

White House Protection Force

Contemporary Romance

Eagle Cove

Henderson's Ranch*

Where Dreams

Action-Adventure Thrillers

Dead Chef

Miranda Chase Origin

Science Fiction / Fantasy

Deities Anonymous

Other
The Future Night Stalkers
Single Titles

ABOUT THIS BOOK

Emily Beale, sixteen years old, faces her first major flight as a student pilot. The dramatic moment of the "first solo" isn't what defines a young pilot. It's the four-hour, solo, "cross-country" challenge that determines who they can become.

As Emily flies around Washington's Olympic Mountains and along the Oregon Coast, she discovers that her future just might be on a clearer flight path than she thought possible. If she's ready for it.

Special Thanks

To fan Johanna R. for the story idea. I'm hoping I achieved what you asked for.

1

23 YEARS AGO
BOEING FIELD, SEATTLE, WA

"CLEARED FOR STRAIGHT-OUT NORTH DEPARTURE."

"Roger, Tower. Helo Papa Bravo departing north." Emily Beale eased up on the Robinson R22's collective with her left hand and the small helicopter shuffled into a tentative hover. It was a little skittish until she nudged the cyclic joystick between her knees forward, then it found its stride.

Rising into the air, it transitioned from some slightly bogus blob of a machine with drooping sad-sack rotors to being what it was meant to be.

Emily briefly wondered what that felt like. She was sixteen and had no idea at all of what she was meant to be. Wasn't she supposed to know by now? So many of her overachieving friends back in DC absolutely knew. Or were convinced they did. It felt like she should know. As if.

The two rotor blades dug into the sky with a soft thump-thump barely louder than the humming engine. The school provided very good headsets on their aircraft that cut out almost all of the noise. She felt more than heard the helicopter's performance as a steady thrum through her nervous system.

She could also feel Ken, her flight instructor, watching her from the shadows of the hangar, and barely managed to not look back over her shoulder.

Ten feet up, she nosed forward and eased out of the helicopter parking area, turning for the threshold of Runway 14L. One of Boeing's big jets was taxiing down to the far end of the runway. It would be a good idea to not be anywhere in the vicinity when it took off. Definitely time to get outta here.

Once she was above the runway, she nosed forward and rode up on the collective until she was racing above the tarmac no helicopter needed. The R22 could land or depart from any open area more than thirty feet across. Helicopters so outclassed airplanes.

The morning sun was well-risen and she raced along with her shadow chasing just ahead of her down the grassy median to the west.

"That's it, baby." A line of big commercial jets were parked in front of the monstrous hangars to her left. It's where Boeing performed a lot of their tests and upgrades. She'd take her little Robinson any day.

"What's that?" The Boeing Field air traffic controller called out. Without meaning to, she'd triggered the microphone as she spoke.

"Helo Papa Bravo. Continuing departure," she covered as well as she could. In the future she'd keep her mouth shut.

"Roger. Cleared to one-five thousand."

There may have been a chuckle there.

"One-five thousand. Thank you, Tower." She hated how clearly she'd just labeled herself as a student pilot.

Well, that ended right now. She double-checked the angle of departure and corrected it so that she wasn't at one-three-eight degrees, but *precisely* on the same one-four-zero as Runway 14.

Besides this was the time to do it truly right.

Today was the big flight, the one she'd been waiting for.

For over thirty hours she'd either flown with an instructor in the left seat or locally by herself to practice skills, skills that were already becoming like a second skin.

Now, finally, it was time for her first solo cross-country flight. Not *across* the country, at least not yet. Today it was just her and her two-seat helicopter, winging their way over the Pacific Northwest. A four-hour, four-hundred-mile flight that had to include at least three landings before returning to Boeing Field. It was a test of navigation, control, and endurance.

The freedom of it was heady, but she couldn't afford a mistake. So she held her heading and her rate-of-climb at precisely a hundred and three percent of RPM per the Pilot's Operating Handbook. Nearing her clearance altitude, Emily eased down on the collective in a smooth roll that ended just as the altimeter dial touched fifteen hundred feet. Nailed it.

Below her, Seattle unfolded. The southern industrial area surrounding the airport gave way to a pair of giant sports stadiums and then the towering buildings perched on the steep slope of the city.

Her father, Stephen Beale was down there, on a one-year assignment as the director of FBI-Seattle. She hadn't even mentioned the flying until last night. He'd barely raised an eyebrow when she mentioned she had a big flight the next day.

In the future, she'd keep her goals to herself.

Her dreams seemed to work better that way.

2

By the time she was four, Emily knew her role in life.

Helen Cartwright Magnusson Beale had left no doubts, sparing no effort in grooming her only child for the part.

Ballet from the time she could walk. Piano from age four.

She been too young for the Farrah Fawcett-hair generation, but her mother had tried almost everything else.

At least until Emily had seen Britt Ekland in *The Man with the Golden Gun.*

Despite her father being a prominent member of the FBI, or perhaps because he was, he had a weakness for the silliness of James Bond movies—his only vice that she knew of. It was also the only time she ever heard him laugh louder than an indulgent chuckle. As watching them with Father was one of her few escapes from Mother's relentless schedule, she came to know them intimately.

When she'd first seen Britt, and loved that they had the same light-blonde hair and blue eye color, she'd put her foot down. She'd only been seven but she'd put it down hard.

Straight, shoulder-length, center-part, unhighlighted, and unfoofed. From that day, she'd refused to wear her hair any other way. When Mother had told her that it wasn't up to her, Emily had raised her palm and said, "Talk to the hand." It was one of her prouder moments.

It also had been one of her *few* successful challenges against Mother's wishes. Even though she was now sixteen, Helen would still tell her friends, "Emily, the dear, needs her little rebellions. She'll grow out of them soon."

And they would all nod knowingly. Not.

The elite of the Washington, DC social set wouldn't dare disagree with Helen Cartwright Magnusson Beale. She commanded it as few others did—invitations to her elegant parties were the ultimate "get" of the DC season. Even Father flew home for those. She'd visited him in Seattle just once and that had been sufficient for her.

For herself, Emily had wrangled a month's invitation to live with her father in Seattle. He had warned her that he'd be busy, which had been perfect. Also, the trip was probably all that had prevented there from being a death in the family this summer—either Mother or she herself wouldn't have survived it.

It had left her free to work on a "gift" of her own for Mother.

3

A HELICOPTER LICENSE REQUIRED FORTY HOURS OF FLYING time, plus ground school. Leaving a week's buffer for the flight exam, she flew a minimum of two hours a day from the day after her arrival in Seattle.

Yes, a gift that would be a surprise for Mother like nothing she'd ever imagined.

Good girls don't fly oily mechanical things like helicopters themselves, Mother had dismissed the idea not with malice, but with utter disbelief that the only daughter of Helen Cartwright Magnusson Beale would even consider such a male thing as being a pilot. Mother wasn't above riding in them, but "others" flew them.

And this summer, when she and Father crossed paths in his apartment?

Exploring Seattle, had been her easy answer. Yeah, exploring every aspect of its airspace.

She crossed the width of Puget Sound at its narrowest point. The sunlight sparkled off the water and painted the glaciers of the Olympic Mountains a brilliant white. It was a crystalline blue day, perfect weather for such a long training flight.

Just two-point-four miles over water from the West Point lighthouse north of the city to Bainbridge Island. Now, safely over land once more, she automatically began keeping an eye out for safe places to land in case of engine failure.

Also clear of Seattle's airspace restrictions, she climbed to her planned flight profile of five thousand feet. It might be seventy degrees on the ground, but a mile high, it was a chilly forty-three. Until this moment she'd been too busy to notice the chill that almost made her shiver. She set the cabin heater to compensate, then looked ahead.

North.

North up to Port Angeles, that was the first leg of today's flight. The heavy green of Douglas fir forest softened the rolling hills beneath her. Ken had made her promise that she wouldn't go poking into the Olympic National Forest airspace.

But that didn't mean she wasn't going to hug the perimeter of it.

The forest was well over a half-million acres, a thousand square miles of mountainous terrain that averaged over two hundred inches of rain a year—eighteen feet of water to DC's three. It strained the limits of her imagination. She hadn't had time to visit here, so she'd plotted her flight to circle it. Over twenty peaks were higher than her one mile up. It had whole areas of three-hundred-foot tall trees, active glaciers, and moss-dripping rain forest.

It made her want to fly in there, swoop low enough to

really look at, even dive through valleys and circle mountain peaks.

But you didn't mess with the instructions that a man like Ken Kastner gave you, so she stayed clear of the forest, following Highway 101 as a visual flight aid to her circumnavigation.

She'd found Ken by asking who their best pilot was—not best instructor, but best pilot. Twenty years with the US Army's 101st Airborne, Lt. Colonel (retired) Ken Kastner was far and away their best.

Emily had become infatuated with flying after taking a flight with her father. She'd flown with her parents any number of times before, but when she was fifteen, the pilot had invited her to sit in the vacant copilot's seat of an Augusta Westland AW119 Koala. Because it was the VIP version, there was an isolation wall between the passengers and the two forward seats.

Without Mother being able to see, the pilot had let her trace her hands on the controls as he flew them from DC to New York for one of her father's meetings.

That had done it for her.

Ken Kastner was gruff, painfully strict, and flew in ways that she couldn't even comprehend—but had spent many quiet hours flying solo trying to replicate. He was a magician in flight.

When she wasn't in the air, or studying the books, she was exploring every building she could get into around Boeing Field, including many hours in The Museum of Flight.

Haunting The Aviator's Store had become a lunchtime ritual. After her first flight of the day, rain or shine, she'd go for a 10K run around the field's perimeter road. The store and the Blue Max Steakhouse were exactly opposite the helicopter school's midfield hangar, but she couldn't cross the middle of the airport unless she flew...and she didn't think the tower would appreciate her daily flights back and forth across the midfield.

The rest of the time she'd hung out with the pilots, collecting every tidbit and story she could.

She'd hated using Mother's social skills—but they were a formidable weapon, so Emily felt forced to borrow from lessons she'd learned since toddlerhood.

How to fit in perfectly?

Slacks to jeans. A Lord & Taylor blouse to an "I'd rather be flying" t-shirt. Anne Klein flats to sturdy REI walking shoes.

Thankfully, she'd scouted the place and shifted her wardrobe before her first day.

Throwing them a lunchtime barbeque as a "get to know them" event had seemed over the top. It was something her mother almost assuredly would have done just to show precisely who was in control. Who had the "funds."

Instead, she brought in a big box of donuts, and was welcome ever after.

They were a huge hit and it was hard, but she shrugged off the few questions about where she'd bought them. Admitting that she'd made them herself would cast her in some "other" role than flier and she didn't want that.

There was a time she'd thought to be a chef. Right up until that first flight at fifteen, in the copilot's seat.

Growing up in DC, with Father so often at work, she'd escaped into the family kitchen. Clarice, their French chef, was as strict as Ken in many ways. If Emily was in the kitchen, then she was going to learn how to cook. She could now make donuts for ten or a seven-course meal for thirty centered around Boeuf Bourguignon or pâté stuffed goose.

Mother had conceded that her cooking was an acceptable pastime—for now.

Helen Cartwright Magnusson Beale couldn't scramble an egg.

4

HER FIRST STOP WAS AT FAIRCHILD INTERNATIONAL Airport in Port Angeles. It seemed a very grand name for an airport that had no control tower and averaged barely seventy flights a day—Boeing averaged over five hundred and the nearby Sea-Tac over twelve hundred.

It was the first airport she'd be landing at on her own that she and Ken hadn't already gone to before. Somehow it was too easy, as if she was doing it wrong, though she couldn't think of what else to do.

She listened to the automated weather at the frequency listed on her chart. Called her approach on the airport's general frequency, and flew the pattern...to land neatly by the tiny office building. The airport didn't even rate a diner or a pie shop—one of the main attractions to most fliers during a weekend jaunt.

No, this wasn't her big stop. And it was so early in the flight, she didn't even get out to stretch her legs. But she'd pulled it off, Ken might have acknowledged the achievement with a nod. Then again, he wasn't much given to compliments.

After the Robinson had idled for a minute, she felt its impatience to be underway as well. Reversing the process, she was soon aloft, out of the pattern, and continuing west across the top of the Olympic Peninsula.

To her right, across the ten miles of the Strait of San Juan de Fuca rose Vancouver Island.

Ken had talked a little about long flights over open water. It had seemed like the safest place to go down: no trees, houses, or uneven terrain to worry about. The Robinson could have water wings, inflatable floats along the skids, though this one didn't.

Damn inflatables create a lot of air drag, slow you down, burns more fuel, more time over the water. Besides, first big wave tips you and you catch a spinning rotor you're toast anyway. Instead, when your belly hits, you roll hard left to drive the rotor blades into the water to stop them. Then you climb out the right-hand door and get away as fast as you can. If you're lucky, you're alive. Unless that's unlucky because you were dumb enough to be out there flying without a second bird.

It was a different type of thinking.

Civilians would need time to panic, unbuckle, and exit the helo.

Ken's attitude was, *This is reality, deal with it.*

Emily would stick with the challenges of the thick forest, and keep following the highway...for now.

5

Her first real stop was two and a half hours out of Boeing in Astoria, Oregon. Here she could stretch, and refill her fuel tanks. The airport was big enough to actually have fuel.

Still nowhere to eat, but that was okay. Astoria Airport might be livelier than Fairchild, with a hundred flights a day, but it was a very different mix.

To her left were the helicopters for the Bar pilots. They were the pilots who specialized in transiting ships over the massive turbulence created by the Columbia River slamming into the Pacific Ocean. Most pilots were delivered across the Columbia River Bar by high-performance patrol boats, but some had to be flown to and from their ships.

Even as she waited, an Aérospatiale MH-65 Dolphin in US Coast Guard colors rolled out of the hangar to her right.

She waved, and the copilot waved back as they taxied

past. She might be flying a tiny Robinson R22, but there was a community of being a helo pilot.

Of course, the Dolphin cost thirty times what her rented helicopter did. And she couldn't get over its beauty. It moved with an effortless declaration of, "I'm going to a rescue, so stay out of my way."

Emily refilled her water bottle, used the ladies, and hit a vending machine for a Snickers while they were filling up the grand fifteen gallons of avgas she'd burned so far. By careful planning, she was just under thirty miles from the range limit for full tanks—not counting the thirty-minute reserve.

Without her noticing, somewhere between Fairchild and Astoria, all this had become normal. Not complacent; Ken would ground her without hesitation if she did that for a single second.

No.

But it had become...familiar.

Watch the terrain. Note possible emergency landing spots. Scan for other air traffic. Sweep the instruments.

She'd had the collective trimmed in tightly enough that she didn't really need to keep her left hand on the control all the time, though she did anyway. The feeling of absolute connection to the machine let her focus on other things.

If Ken signed off on it, she'd have more than enough hours to take the test next week. She'd be seventeen tomorrow—had to be at least that to get her private pilot's license—not that anyone would notice her birthday out here. Mother would have held a formal tea, thick with future-eligible young men, of course. Or perhaps not, simply using it as an excuse to find more things about her daughter that weren't "sufficient to a girl of your breeding." Better to have no party at all.

Emily had already passed the ground school test. For lack of anything else to read, she was studying the textbook for instrument flying, starting on the next license would be birthday present enough.

That's what was puzzling.

The *next* license?

When would she ever get to fly after she returned to DC?

She paid the fueler and climbed back into the helo within two minutes of her planned schedule.

Ken was always emphasizing time. *Flights happen on time. Imagine you're a grunt bleeding out after a gun battle. "Oh, we're running a little behind. Be there in fifteen or so." That's a load of horseshit. You give a time? That's when you hit the ground.* Then he'd grimaced in a friendly way. *Of course arriving early just makes you a sitting duck in the gun battle, so not a lot of fun either.*

Emily started the engine. Watched the time, and, at fifteen seconds to her flight plan, she called the tower and received immediate departure clearance.

Three more seconds' hesitation, then she lifted—on schedule to the second. There.

6

THE OREGON COAST WAS UNLIKE THE WASHINGTON ONE.

Once clear of the mountains, Washington had been mostly low-lying hills and long sandy beaches—in some cases dozens of miles long.

As she headed south just a hundred yards off the Oregon Coast, she was soon flying over frequent rocky headlands sometimes so close that they almost touched one another.

Coves of pristine little beaches were tucked away between many of them. Some of the coves would be underwater at high tide, but it was dead low right now and the beaches were plentiful. She wondered how many of them were never visited. Her favorites were the ones scooped out beneath a hundred feet of steep cliff, only a small boat could get into many of them.

A small boat or...

Would Ken give her hell? Or cheer her on?

Before she could think about that too much, she

dumped all lift from the collective. Easing back on the cyclic, she dropped from five thousand feet like a stone.

At five hundred feet, she pulled up on the power. The responsive little Robinson fluttered down through three hundred, two, one—just past the cliff top—and stabilized at seventy. That was perhaps a little close to ditching in the water, but it had worked.

Keeping a close eye on the wet sand, and especially the tips of her rotor blades, she eased onto the beach.

No more than a hundred meters long, it was generous enough that she was at least an hour above the high tide mark when the skids finally settled.

That was longer than she could afford to stay. Ken would notice her late return. And if she was over an hour late without calling the FAA to revise her flight plan, they'd call out a search-and-rescue team on her, which would be totally suck.

The first thing that Emily wished as she stepped out on the pebbled sand was that she'd brought a jacket. The sun was just clearing the headland to illuminate the sea-dark blues and highlight the waves rolling into her little cove and thumping onto the sand. Too bad she'd be gone before the sun reached the sand.

A cool sea fog sent long tendrils into the cove. It was thin, thin enough that she didn't need to worry about visibility, but she'd have to keep an eye on it.

But moments later, she no longer cared about the chill.

The air was thick with the smell of unknown places. The Northern Pacific, the Gulf of Alaska, the Bering Sea and Arctic Ocean, each had added something to the air. A freshness, a crispness, a clarity.

Washington, DC, even the family beach house by Ocean City, always smelled of...money. She didn't know how else to think about it. There never was lemonade or a beer, there was a pleasant chardonnay. A t-shirt was rarely an acceptable alternative to a starched and pressed blouse. Most of the shore traffic was expensive sailboats.

On her long flight down this coast she'd seen only freighters, tankers, and fishermen.

There was an honesty to the Pacific Ocean air. As if she was breathing it at her own risk.

To stretch her legs, she walked to the far end of the little beach.

Sitting on the sand, for the thousandth time since she'd written it last week, she fingered the sealed letter in her back pocket. It was now folded *and* crumpled because her father had surprised her by still being home for breakfast this morning. She took it out each morning to see if she had the nerve to mail it.

Not yet.

Emily smoothed out the envelope.

Vice Admiral James Parker.

Mother had determined that Smith, Brown, or even Bard would be acceptable colleges for her to attend while she was looking for the correct husband. Mother had been a Smith girl. The all-women's college had long been deemed as the prime school for attracting a properly eligible husband. Its graduate list was illustrious: Nancy Reagan, Barbara Bush, even Julia Child. Gloria Steinem was not mentioned in decent company, of course.

Admiral Parker was a long-time friend of her father's. She'd made a point of cooking for him when he visited— he'd always seemed so appreciative of her food. It was a sharp contrast to their family meals: Father who barely seemed to notice what he ate and Mother enjoying another opportunity to give her daughter tips for personal improvement. On his last visit, she'd made him one of her best, a rack of lamb with white truffle sauce.

Again she smoothed the letter that had been little more than a vague idea as recently as last week.

The question inside this envelope would probably give Helen Cartwright Magnusson Beale a stroke. Perhaps that's why Emily had originally written it.

But the idea had grown since then.

There were some schools where you didn't just apply. You had to be nominated, typically by your congressman or senator, but she was a resident of DC. DC didn't have any representative of its own in either part of the congress.

She'd considered asking Father but didn't think she could bear it if he said no, or simply forgot about her request until it was too late, as he sometimes did.

What would Admiral Parker think about such a request? *Oh, that slight, young girl of Stephen's who thinks she knows how to cook. Who does she think she's kidding? Nominate her to United States Military Academy at West Point?*

Still unsure herself of why he would, she folded it carefully and returned it to her pocket.

She was suddenly stiff from sitting on the hard sand, as if she hadn't moved in hours, though less than fifteen minutes had passed.

Reluctant to leave, she allowed herself ten minutes to explore along the line of her earlier footsteps.

The tang of salt and seaweed swirled thickly in the

cove. Great strands of round kelp drew messages she couldn't read along the beach. Stalks of seaweed that looked like baby army-green palm trees were mixed in with flat strands that looked like someone had run a road roller over spinach-and-squid ink linguini.

Mixed into the sand were battered shells. Unlike the East Coast, few of them were bigger than a silver dollar and even the blue mussel shells were mostly shattered. She picked up a few, but dropped them back on the beach.

Most of the way back to the Robinson, she spotted a yellow stone mixed in with all of the dark sea-rounded pebbles. Nearly the size of her thumb, its goldish color appeared to come from just inside the translucent surface.

An agate.

She spooked a sandpiper that had been chasing the tide up and down the beach as she rinsed her discovery in the backwash of a thumping wave—before she too scooted back onto the sand for safety.

The line of sunshine was just reaching the shore—it caught the agate brightly.

When she let it slip into her palm, it just fit. The sea had worn it to the perfect shape so that she could close her hand completely over it, but still feel as if her hand was full.

Emily had never been much given to talismans, but there was something there in the stone that had her slipping it into her pocket beside the letter.

7

THE REST OF THE FLIGHT PASSED EFFORTLESSLY. EMILY HAD thought that the flight would be the challenge, but it wasn't. The flying itself had become easy. The long duration cross-country flight by herself had integrated the helicopter's behavior into all of the knowledge that had already been in her head. Now it was just a part of her body's memory.

Making up for her stop at the beach wasn't wholly impossible. She'd built some slack into her overall schedule, especially on the ground at Hillsboro Airport, just outside Portland, Oregon. There, instead of her planned lunch break, she requested a stop-and-go, and the tower had been willing to oblige. She fully landed in the middle of the runway, then pushed aloft again just seconds later.

Adding that time savings to her planned cruise speed being five miles per hour slower than standard cruise— and maybe pushing that a little on the final long leg back to Seattle—she was only four minutes late returning to Boeing Field.

She'd wanted to be exactly on time, but it had been worth stopping on that beach. There was something there in that luminous gold agate. And something in that letter. Neither of which she understood.

It was only as she was hovering to land back in the exact spot she'd left four hours ago that she saw who was waiting for her, standing beside Ken.

Emily thumped down the last five feet—hard.

8

"Hi, Emily!" He held open the Robinson's door for her.

"Daddy?" She almost didn't recognize him. Not because he was wearing a polo shirt rather than a suit, though that was surprising. It's just that he was so out of place. "What are you doing here?"

"You said this was your big flight, so I thought I should come and see how you did. I got here early so that I wouldn't miss anything." He helped her out of the Robinson, which was good because she couldn't seem to get out of her seat by herself. "Gave me a chance to talk to Ken."

"But..." she didn't know what else to say.

"How did it go?"

"Fine," was the only brilliant comment she could manage for an answer. "How did you find me?"

Her father's look said just how foolish a question that was. He was the director of FBI-Seattle. Maybe even being groomed for the assistant directorship of the FBI itself. *Of course* someone would be keeping tabs on where his family was at all times. Talk about being totally clueless.

Ken held out his hand in a familiar gesture.

She passed over her log book.

He flipped to the latest page. "Fairchild, Astoria, Hillsboro. How long were you on the ground at each?"

"Two minutes, ten minutes, and about five seconds."

He eyed her through his dark sunglasses, "Thought you planned fifteen at HIO. Why were you four minutes late instead of eleven minutes early?" Because Ken would know the exact distances, and that she would hold to her exact planned cruise speed.

Of its own volition her hand slipped into her back pocket to brush against the agate. But instead it found the letter and withdrew it without her really remembering what it was.

"I stopped. At a beach." This time she withdrew the agate. It was like the color of the sun just before it kissed the horizon. She closed her fist around it to remind her that it was... "It was important."

Father and Ken traded some look that she couldn't interpret. Probably that this sixteen-year-old girl was an idiot and should just go back to DC and become like her mommy.

"Time on the beach?" Ken grunted out.

She told him and he nodded.

"How hard did you burn to make up the time?"

Emily hadn't wanted him to know that.

"I ran at five miles per hour above normal cruise. I

ran the fuel calculations and knew my increased burn rate wouldn't threaten my reserve."

"How did you calculate that while flying? You said you were on the ground for just five seconds."

"Maybe it was three. I'd memorized the fuel burn chart and ran the calcs in my head."

Ken harrumphed. "Still, four minutes late. You need to work on that."

Emily nodded and looked down at her feet.

"Jesus, Ken, you're scaring the crap out of her. Sounds like you did great, Emily."

She looked at him to see if he was joking, but he didn't appear to be in a James Bond movie mood.

"No," Ken cut him off. "When a student flies a course like that even within an hour of on-time, that's great. When a pilot of Emily Beale's caliber misses the mark by four minutes, I want to know why."

Emily couldn't seem to find her voice. So instead, she handed over the crumpled envelope.

Ken unfolded it and read the address, "Who the hell is Vice Admiral James Parker?"

"An old family friend," Father answered for her. Then turned, "What's in the letter, Emily?"

"A—" it was going to sound so stupid, but it was what she wanted. Was it? Definitely.

Not in rebellion against her mother.

Instead *for* herself.

She wanted to someday hear another person say "a pilot of Emily Beale's caliber" and mean it just as Ken had.

Emily clamped her hand down hard on the agate,

reaching back for how she'd felt sitting on that beautiful beach. So...free.

"It's a request that he recommend me to West Point."

She couldn't look up to see what anyone's reaction was.

"Chin up, Emily," Father brushed a finger under her chin until she looked at him. "You don't get into a place like West Point by looking down."

She struggled to meet his eyes, then nodded to herself when she'd managed.

"Am I so scary that you couldn't ask me?"

She nodded, even if it wasn't the most tactful thing she'd ever done.

"That'll teach me," he muttered mostly to himself.

"Teach you what?"

He brushed a hand on her hair. "I love your mother very much, don't get me wrong when I say this. But I thought you were growing up to follow in her footsteps, so I saw no reason to interfere."

"Mother makes me *insane!*" Emily slapped a hand over her mouth.

"Only because you're so much alike. Your mother, in addition to being a great beauty, is an exceptionally intelligent and tenacious woman. You got all of those from her."

"But I got your eyes." Emily didn't want to have gotten anything from Helen Cartwright Magnusson Beale, but didn't say so.

"But you got my eyes," he agreed, brushing her hair again as if seeing her for the first time.

At the sound of tearing paper, Emily spun to look at Ken.

He was tearing up her letter.

"Hey! It took me forever to get that right."

He chucked it into a nearby garbage can.

"Let's start again. *I'm* a retired Lieutenant Colonel. I know a general or two who owe me their damned lives. Add in your father, and that's a fair set of recommendations."

"But Admiral Parker—" she waved toward the discarded letter.

Ken, who'd never smiled once in all the time she'd known him, not only smiled, but gave her a sideways hug.

"You're going to do great at the Point. We need pilots like you. We need commanders like you too, so think about that once you're inside."

"Come on, Emily. Let's the three of us talk about this over a birthday dinner. A day early, but does pizza sound good?"

"Sounds awesome!" Father remembering her birthday? Maybe he did see her as more than his wife's daughter.

She looked one last time toward the garbage can. It had taken her so many hours to get that right.

Ken laughed at her in a tone like a grinding cement mixer. "He's a swabbie. No soldier in his right mind is going to listen to a swabbie."

Emily hadn't wanted to follow in her mother's footsteps. Following in Lieutenant Colonel Ken Kastner's sounded far better...but still not quite right.

Maybe—she glanced back at the Robinson now sitting quietly in the afternoon sun after its long flight— maybe, like on the beach, she'd try following in her own.

*Be sure to keep reading to see an excerpt from the exciting
White House Protection Force series.*

IF YOU ENJOYED THAT,

YOU'LL LOVE THE NIGHT STALKERS 5E!

TARGET OF THE HEART (EXCERPT)

MAJOR PETE NAPIER HOVERED HIS MH-47G CHINOOK helicopter ten kilometers outside of Lhasa, Tibet and a mere two inches off the tundra. A mixed action team of Delta Force and The Activity—the slipperiest intel group on the planet—flung themselves aboard.

The additional load sent an infinitesimal shift in the cyclic control in his right hand. The hydraulics to close the rear loading ramp hummed through the entire frame of the massive helicopter. By the time his crew chief could reach forward to slap an "all secure" signal against his shoulder, they were already ten feet up and fifty out. That was enough altitude. He kept the nose down as he clawed for speed in the thin air at eleven thousand feet.

"Totally worth it," one of the D-boys announced as soon as he was on the Chinook's internal intercom.

He'd have to remember to tell that to the two Black Hawks flying guard for him...when they were in a friendly country and could risk a radio transmission. This deep inside China—or rather Chinese-held territory as the CIA's mission-briefing spook had insisted on calling it —radios attracted attention and were only used to avoid imminent death and destruction.

"Great, now I just need to get us out of this alive."

"Do that, Pete. We'd appreciate it."

He wished to hell he had a stealth bird like the one that had gone into bin Laden's compound. But the one that had crashed during that raid had been blown up. Where there was one, there were always two, but the second had gone back into hiding as thoroughly as if it had never existed. He hadn't heard a word about it since.

The Tibetan terrain was amazing, even if all he could see of it was the monochromatic green of night vision. And blackness. The largest city in Tibet lay a mere ten kilometers away and they were flying over barren wilderness. He could crash out here and no one would know for decades unless some yak herder stumbled upon them. Or were yaks in Mongolia? He was a corn-fed, white boy from Colorado, what did he know about Tibet? Most of the countries he'd flown into on Black Ops missions he'd only seen at night anyway.

While moving very, very fast.

Like now.

The inside of his visor was painted with overlapping readouts. A pre-defined terrain map, the best that modern satellite imaging could build made the first layer. This wasn't some crappy, on-line, look-at-a-picture-of-your-house display. Someone had a pile of dung outside their goat pen? He could see it, tell you how high it was, and probably say if they were pygmy goats or full-size LaManchas by the size of their shit-pellets if he zoomed in.

On top of that were projected the forward-looking infrared camera images. The FLIR imaging gave him a real-time overlay, in case someone had put an addition onto their goat shed since the last satellite pass or parked their tractor across his intended flight path.

His nervous system was paying autonomic attention to that combined landscape. He also compensated for the thin air at altitude as he instinctively chose when to start his climb over said goat shed or his swerve around it.

It was the third layer, the tactical display that had most of his attention. At least he and the two Black Hawks flying escort on him were finally on the move.

To insert this deep into Tibet, without passing over Bhutan or Nepal, they'd had to add wingtanks on the Black Hawks' hardpoints where he'd much rather have a couple banks of Hellfire missiles. Still, they had 20 mm chain guns and the crew chiefs had miniguns which was some comfort. His twin-rotor Chinook might be the biggest helicopter that the Night Stalkers flew, but it was the cargo van of Special Operations and only had two miniguns and a machine gun of its own. Though he'd put his three crew chiefs up against the best Black Hawk shooter any day.

While the action team was busy infiltrating the capital city and gathering intelligence on the particularly brutal Chinese assistant administrator, Pete and his crews had been squatting out in the wilderness under a camouflage net designed to make his helo look like just another god-forsaken Himalayan lump of granite.

Command had determined that it was better for the helos to wait on site through the day than risk flying out and back in. He and his crew had stood shifts on guard duty, but none of them had slept. They'd been flying together too long to have any new jokes, so they'd played a lot of cribbage. He'd long ago ruled no gambling on a mission, after a fistfight had broken out about a bluff hand that cost a Marine three hundred and forty-seven dollars. Marines hated losing to Army no matter how many times it happened. They'd had to sit on him for a long time before he calmed down.

Tonight's mission was part of an on-going campaign to discredit the Chinese "presence" in Tibet on the international stage—as if occupying the country the last sixty-plus years didn't count toward ruling, whether invited or not. As usual, there was a crucial vote coming up at the U.N.—that, as usual, the Chinese could be guaranteed to ignore. However, the ever-hopeful CIA was in a hurry to make sure that any damaging information that they could validate was disseminated as thoroughly as possible prior to the vote.

Not his concern.

His concern was, were they going to pass over some Chinese sentry post at their top speed of a hundred and ninety-six miles an hour? The sentries would then call down a couple Shenyang J-16 jet fighters that could hustle along at Mach 2—over fifteen *hundred* mph—to fry his sorry ass. He knew there was a pair of them parked at Lhasa along with some older gear that would be just as effective against his three helos.

"Don't suppose you could get a move on, Pete?"

"Eat shit, Nicolai!" He was a good man to have as a copilot. Pete knew he was holding on too tight, and Nicolai knew that a joke was the right way to ease the moment.

He, Nicolai, and the four pilots in the two Black Hawks had a long way to go tonight and he'd never make it if he stayed so tight on the controls that he could barely maneuver. Pete eased off and felt his fingers tingle with the rush of returning blood. They dove down into gorges and followed them as long as they dared. They hugged cliff walls at every opportunity to decrease their radar profile. And they climbed.

That was the true danger—they would be up near the helos' limits when they crossed over the backbone of the Himalayas in their rush for India. The air was so rarefied that they burned fuel at a prodigious rate. Their reserve didn't allow for any extended battles while crossing the border...not for any battle at all really.

IT WAS PITCH DARK OUTSIDE HER HELICOPTER WHEN Captain Danielle Delacroix stamped on the left rudder pedal while giving the big Chinook right-directed control on the cyclic. It tipped her most of the way onto her side but let her continue in a straight line. A Chinook's rotors were sixty feet across—front to back they overlapped to make the spread a hundred feet long. By cross-controlling her bird to tip it, she managed to execute a straight line between two mock pylons only thirty feet apart. They were made of thin cloth so they wouldn't down the helo if you sliced one—she was the only trainee to not have cut one yet.

At her current angle of attack, she took up less than a half-rotor of width, just twenty-four feet. That left her nearly three feet to either side, sufficient as she was moving at under a hundred knots.

The training instructor sitting beside her in the copilot's seat didn't react as she swooped through the training course at Fort Campbell, Kentucky. Only child of a single mother, she was used to providing her own feedback loops, so she didn't expect anything else. Those who expected outside validation rarely survived the SOAR induction testing, never mind the two years of training that followed.

As a loner kid, Danielle had learned that self-motivated congratulations and fun were much easier to come by than external ones. She'd spent innumerable hours deep in her mind as a pre-teen superheroine. At twenty-nine she was well on her way to becoming a real life one, though Helo-girl had never been a character she'd thought of in her youth.

External validation or not, after two years of training with the U.S. Army's 160th Special Operations Aviation Regiment she was ready for some action. At least *she* was convinced that she was. But the trainers of Fort Campbell, Kentucky had not signed off on anyone in her trainee class yet. Nor had they given any hint of when they might.

She ducked ten tons of racing Chinook under a bridge and bounced into a near vertical climb to clear the power line on the far side. Like a ride on the toboggan at Terrassee Dufferin during *Le Carnaval de Québec,* only with ten thousand horsepower at her fingertips. Using her Army signing bonus—the first money in her life that was truly hers—to attend *Le Carnaval* had been her one trip back to her birthplace since her mother took them to America when she was ten.

To even apply to SOAR required five years of prior military rotorcraft experience. She had applied after seven years because of a chance encounter—or rather what she'd thought was a chance encounter at the time.

Captain Justin Roberts had been a top Chinook pilot, the one who had convinced her to switch from her beloved Black Hawk and try out the massive twin-rotor craft. One flight and she'd been a goner, begging her commander until he gave in and let her cross over to the new platform. Justin had made the jump from the 10th Mountain Division to the 160th SOAR not long after that.

Then one night she'd been having pizza in Watertown, New York a couple miles off the 10th's base at Fort Drum.

"Danielle?" Justin had greeted her with the surprise of finding a good friend in an unexpected place. Danielle had always liked Justin—even if he was a too-tall, too-handsome cowboy and completely knew it. But "good friend" was unusual for Danielle, with anyone, and Justin came close.

"Captain Roberts," as a dry greeting over the top edge of her Suzanne Brockmann novel didn't faze him in the slightest.

"Mind if I join ya?" A question he then answered for himself by sliding into the opposite seat and taking a slice of her pizza. She been thinking of taking the leftovers back to base, but that was now an idle thought.

"Are you enjoying life in SOAR?" she did her best to appear a normal, social human, a skill she'd learned by rote. *Greeting someone you knew after a time apart? Ask a question about them.* "They treating you well?"

"Whoo-ee, you have no idea, Danielle," his voice was smooth as...well, always...so she wouldn't think about it also sounding like a pickup line. He was beautiful but didn't interest her; the outgoing ones never did.

"Tell me." *Men love to talk about themselves, so let them.*

And he did. But she'd soon forgotten about her novel and would have forgotten the pizza if he hadn't reminded her to eat.

His stories shifted from intriguing to fascinating. There was a world out there that she'd been only peripherally aware of. The Night Stalkers of the 160th SOAR weren't simply better helicopter pilots, they were the most highly-trained and best-equipped ones anywhere. Their missions were pure razor's edge and Black Op dark.

He'd left her with a hundred questions and enough interest to fill out an application to the 160th Special Operations Aviation Regiment (airborne). Being a decent guy, Justin even paid for the pizza after eating half.

The speed at which she was rushed into testing told her that her meeting with Justin hadn't been by chance and that she owed him more than half a pizza next time they met. She'd asked after him a couple of times since she'd made it past the qualification exams—and the examiners' brutal interviews that had left her questioning her sanity, never mind her ability.

"Justin Roberts is presently deployed, ma'am," was the only response she'd ever gotten.

Now that she was through training—almost, had to be soon, didn't it?—Danielle realized that was probably less of an evasion and more likely to do with the brutal op tempo the Night Stalkers maintained. The SOAR 1st Battalion had just won the coveted Lt. General Ellis D. Parker awards for Outstanding Combat Aviation Battalion *and* Aviation Battalion of the Year. They'd been on deployment every single day of the last year, actually of the last decade-plus since 9/11.

The very first Special Forces boots on the ground in Afghanistan were delivered that October by the Night Stalkers and nothing had slacked off since. Justin might be in the 5th battalion D company, but they were just as heavily assigned as the 1st.

Part of the recruits' training had included tours in Afghanistan. But unlike their prior deployments, these were brief, intense, and then they'd be back in the States pushing to integrate their new skills.

SOAR needed her training to end and so did she.

Danielle was ready for the job, in her own, inestimable opinion. But she wasn't going to get there until the trainers signed off that she'd reached fully mission-qualified proficiency. FMQ was the gold star of the Night Stalkers pipeline.

The Fort Campbell training course was never set up the same from one flight to the next, but it always had a time limit. The time would be short and they didn't tell you what it was. So she drove the Chinook for all it was worth like Regina Jaquess waterskiing her way to U.S. Ski Team Female Athlete of the Year.

The Night Stalkers were a damned secretive lot, and after two years of training, she understood why. With seven years flying for the 10th, she'd thought she was good.

She'd been repeatedly lauded as one of the top pilots at Fort Drum.

The Night Stalkers had offered an education in what it really meant to fly. In the two years of training, she'd flown more hours than in the seven years prior, despite two deployments to Iraq. And spent more time in the classroom than her life-to-date accumulated flight hours.

But she was ready now. It was *très viscérale,* right down in her bones she could feel it. The Chinook was as much a part of her nervous system as breathing.

Too bad they didn't build men the way they built the big Chinooks—especially the MH-47G which were built specifically to SOAR's requirements. The aircraft were steady, trustworthy, and the most immensely powerful helicopters deployed in the U.S. Army—what more could a girl ask for? But finding a superhero man to go with her superhero helicopter was just a fantasy for a lonely girl who'd once had dreams of more.

She dove down into a canyon and slid to a hover mere inches over the reservoir inside the thirty-second window laid out on the flight plan.

Danielle resisted a sigh. She was ready for something to happen and to happen soon.

PETE'S CHINOOK AND HIS TWO ESCORT BLACK HAWKS crossed into the mountainous province of Sikkim, India ten feet over the glaciers and still moving fast. It was an hour before dawn, they'd made it out of China while it was still dark.

"Thirty minutes of fuel remaining," Nicolai said it like a personal challenge when they hit the border.

"Thanks, I never would have noticed."

It had been a nail-biting tradeoff: the more fuel he burned, the more easily he climbed due to the lighter load. The more he climbed, the faster he burned what little fuel remained.

Safe in Indian airspace he climbed hard as Nicolai counted down the minutes remaining, burning fuel even faster than he had been while crossing the mountains of southern Tibet. They caught up with the U.S. Air Force HC-130P Combat King refueling tanker with only ten minutes of fuel left.

"Ram that bitch," Nicolai called out.

Pete extended the refueling probe which reached only a few feet beyond the forward edge of the rotor blade and drove at the basket trailing behind the tanker on its long hose.

He nailed it on the first try despite the fluky winds. Striking the valve in the basket with over four hundred pounds of pressure, a clamp snapped over the refueling probe and Jet A fuel shot into his tanks.

His helo had the least fuel due to having the most men aboard, so he was first in line. His Number Two picked up the second refueling basket trailing off the other wing of the Combat King. Thirty seconds and three hundred gallons later and he was breathing much more easily.

"Ah," Nicolai sighed. "It is better than the sex," his thick Russian accent only ever surfaced in this moment or in a bar while picking up women.

"Hey, Nicolai," Nicky the Greek called over the

intercom from his crew chief position seated behind Pete. "Do you make love in Russian?"

A question Pete had always been careful to avoid.

"For you, I make special exception." That got a laugh over the system.

Which explained why Pete always kept his mouth shut at this moment.

"The ladies, Nicolai? What about the ladies?" Alfie the portside gunner asked.

"Ah," he sighed happily as he signaled that the other helos had finished their refueling and formed up to either side, "the ladies love the Russian. They don't need to know I grew up in Maryland and I learn my great-great-grandfather's native tongue at the University called Virginia."

He sounded so pleased that Pete wished he'd done the same rather than study Japanese and Mandarin.

Another two hours of—Thank God—straight-and-level flight at altitude through the breaking dawn and they landed on the aircraft carrier awaiting them in the Bay of Bengal. India had agreed to turn a blind eye as long as the Americans never actually touched their soil.

Once standing on the deck—and the worst of the kinks had been worked out—he pulled his team together: six pilots and seven crew chiefs.

"Honor to serve!" He saluted them sharply.

"Hell yeah!" They shouted in unison and saluted in turn. It was their version of spiking the football in the end zone.

A petty officer in a bright green vest appeared at his elbow, "Follow me please, sir." He pointed toward the Navy-gray command structure that towered above the carrier's deck. The rear admiral of the entire carrier strike group was waiting for him just outside the entrance. Not a good idea to keep a one-star waiting, so he waved at the team.

"See you in the mess for dinner," he shouted to the crew over the noise of an F-18 Hornet fighter jet trapping on the #2 wire. After two days of surviving on MREs while squatting on the Tibetan tundra, he was ready for a steak, a burger, a mountain of pasta, whatever. Or maybe all three.

The green escorted him across the hazards of the busy flight deck. Pete had kept his helmet on to buffer the noise, but even at that he winced as another Hornet fired up and was flung aloft by the catapult.

"Orders, Major Napier," the Rear Admiral handed him a folded sheet the moment he arrived. "Hate to lose you." He saluted, which Pete automatically returned before looking down at the sheet of paper in his hands. The man was gone before the import of Pete's orders slammed in.

A different green-clad deckhand showed up with Pete's duffle bag and began guiding him toward a loading C-2 Greyhound twin-prop airplane. It was parked Number Two for the launch catapult, close behind the raised jet-blast deflector.

His crew, being led across in the opposite direction to return to the berthing decks below, looked at him aghast.

"Stateside," was all he managed to gasp out as they passed.

A stream of foul cursing followed him from behind. Their crew was tight. Why the hell was Command breaking it up?

And what in the name of fuck-all had he done to deserve this?

He glanced at the orders again as he stumbled up the Greyhound's rear ramp and crash landed into a seat.

Training rookies?

It was worse than a demotion.

This was punishment.

Keep reading at fine retailers everywhere:
Target of the Heart

ABOUT THE AUTHOR

USA Today and Amazon #1 Bestseller M. L. "Matt" Buchman started writing on a flight south from Japan to ride his bicycle across the Australian Outback. Just part of a solo around-the-world trip that ultimately launched his writing career.

From the very beginning, his powerful female heroines insisted on putting character first, *then* a great adventure. He's since written over 60 action-adventure thrillers and military romantic suspense novels. And just for the fun of it: 100 short stories, and a fast-growing pile of read-by-author audiobooks.

Booklist says: "3X Top 10 of the Year." PW says: "Tom Clancy fans open to a strong female lead will clamor for more." His fans say: "I want more now...of everything." That his characters are even more insistent than his fans is a hoot.

As a 30-year project manager with a geophysics degree who has designed and built houses, flown and jumped out of planes, and solo-sailed a 50' ketch, he is awed by what is possible. More at: www.mlbuchman.com.

Other works by M. L. Buchman:

Contemporary Romance (cont)

Where Dreams
Where Dreams are Born
Where Dreams Reside
Where Dreams Are of Christmas*
Where Dreams Unfold
Where Dreams Are Written

Science Fiction / Fantasy

Deities Anonymous
Cookbook from Hell: Reheated
Saviors 101

Single Titles
The Nara Reaction
Monk's Maze
the Me and Elsie Chronicles

Non-Fiction

Strategies for Success
Managing Your Inner Artist/Writer
Estate Planning for Authors*
Character Voice
Narrate and Record Your Own
Audiobook*

Short Story Series by M. L. Buchman:

Romantic Suspense

Delta Force
Th Delta Force Shooters
The Delta Force Warriors

Firehawks
The Firehawks Lookouts
The Firehawks Hotshots
The Firebirds

The Night Stalkers
The Night Stalkers
The Night Stalkers 5E
The Night Stalkers CSAR
The Night Stalkers Wedding Stories

US Coast Guard

White House Protection Force

Contemporary Romance

Eagle Cove

Henderson's Ranch*

Where Dreams

Action-Adventure Thrillers

Dead Chef

Miranda Chase Origin

Science Fiction / Fantasy

Deities Anonymous

Other
The Future Night Stalkers
Single Titles

SIGN UP FOR M. L. BUCHMAN'S NEWSLETTER TODAY

and receive:
Release News
Free Short Stories
a Free Book

Get your free book today. Do it now.
free-book.mlbuchman.com